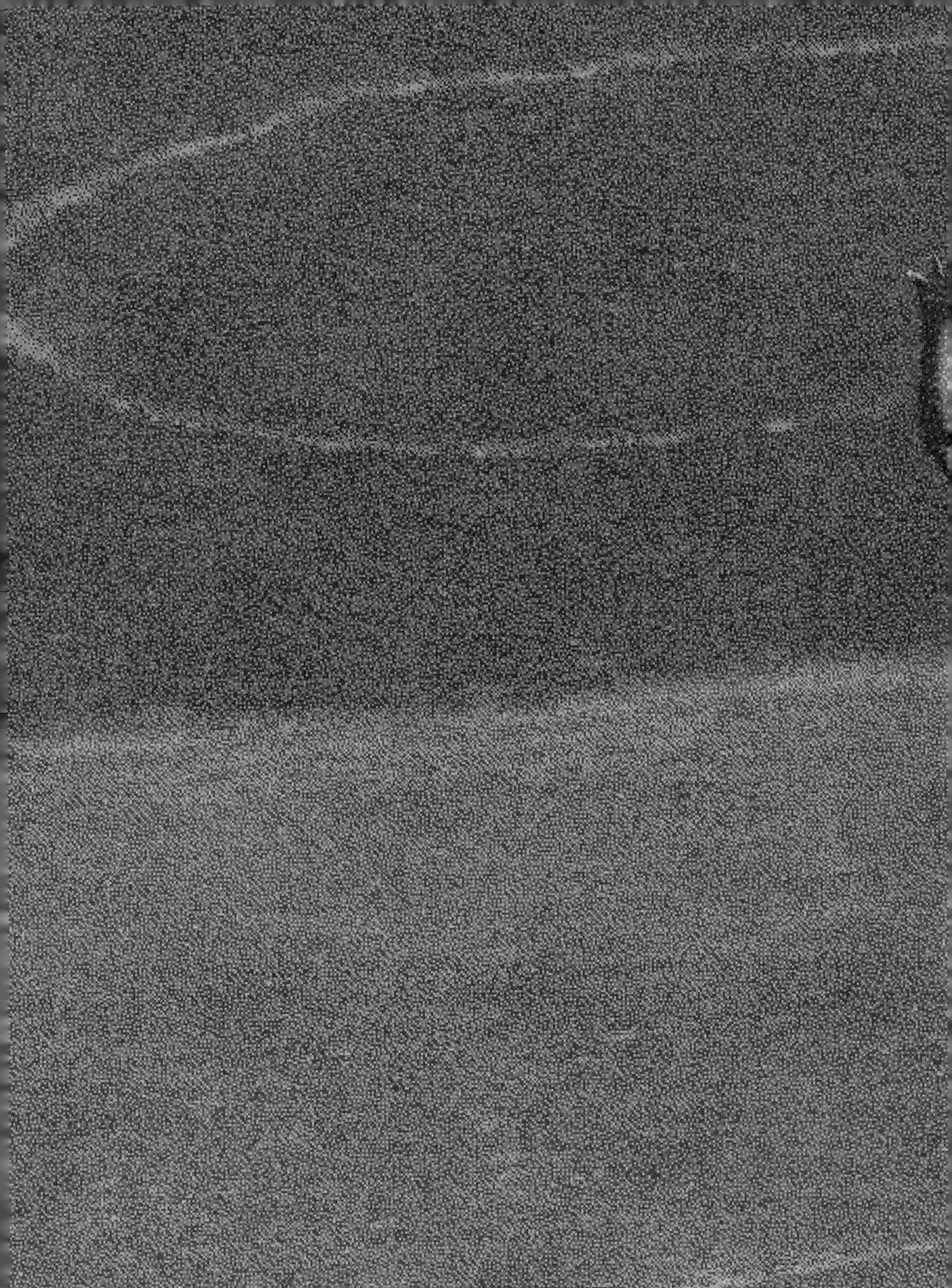

CREATIVE EDUCATION

CHICAGO

WHITE SOX

AL WEST

RICHARD RAMBECK

Published by Creative Education, Inc.

123 S. Broad Street, Mankato, Minnesota 56001

Art Director, Rita Marshall
Cover and title page design by Virginia Evans
Cover and title page illustration by Rob Day
Type set by FinalCopy Electronic Publishing
Book design by Rita Marshall

Photos by Allsport, Duomo, Focus on Sports,
Sportschrome, UPI/Bettmann
and Wide World Photos

Library of Congress Cataloging-in-Publication Data

Rambeck, Richard.

  The Chicago White Sox / by Richard Rambeck.
  p.   cm.
  Summary: A team history of one of Chicago's two
major league baseball teams, the American League's
White Sox, founded by Charles Albert Comiskey in
1901.
  ISBN 0-88682-448-6
  1. Chicago White Sox (Baseball team)—History—
Juvenile literature.   [1. Chicago White Sox (Baseball
team)—History.   2. Baseball—History.]   I. Title.
GV875.C58R36 1991   91-2479
796.357'64'0977311—dc20   CIP

THE EARLY YEARS

With the exception of New York, no U.S. city has played a larger role in this country's economy than Chicago. The metropolis known as "Second City" and the "Windy City" grew from a village of a little more than twenty-nine thousand in 1850 to a huge urban area with more than 3.6 million residents in 1950. Until recently Chicago was the second-largest city in the United States, but it is now third behind New York and Los Angeles.

Located on the southern tip of Lake Michigan in the northern part of Illinois, Chicago is a major water port, as well as a hub of railroad and airplane transportation. Chicago's O'Hare International Airport is the busiest in the United States, handling more than sixty million airline passengers a year.

Chicago greats Eddie Cicotte (left) and Clarence Rowland.

1 9 0 1

On April 24, the first official AL game was played in Chicago as Ray Patterson defeated Cleveland, 8–2.

Chicago also has a rich history, one that is reflected in the many museums located in the city. Included in that rich history is a love for baseball, our national pastime. Chicagoans have flocked to ballparks for more than one hundred years to watch professional baseball. The "Second City" has been able to support not one, but two major-league baseball teams throughout the twentieth century. This is the story of Chicago's American League franchise, the White Sox, a team that is based on the South Side of the city.

The White Sox were among the charter members of the American League, which commenced play in 1901. The team was one of the top clubs in the league at first. Chicago, led by manager Clark Calvin Griffith and star player Fielder Jones, won the first American League pennant with an 83–53 record. (There was no World Series played that year; the American and National league champions didn't start meeting in postseason competition until 1903.) Five years later Chicago was the site of the first intra-city World Series, which featured the National League champion Chicago Cubs and the American League pennant-winning White Sox.

The battle of Chicago was won by the South Siders four games to two, thanks to the pitching of Frank "Yip" Owens, Nick Altrock, and "Doc" White. White Sox owner Charles Comiskey was so thrilled with his team's performance, he awarded the players and coaches a total of fifteen thousand dollars in bonuses. Comiskey, however, would not be so generous with his money in the future.

Former White Sox star Ivan Calderon.

SHOELESS JOE AND THE BLACK SOX SCANDAL

Comiskey Park opened on July 1 to a full house but Chicago lost to St. Louis, 2–0.

After winning the 1906 World Series, the White Sox weren't able to maintain a high level of excellence. They became a middle-of-the-pack club in the eight-team American League and remained one until 1915, when a new manager and a new star joined the team. The manager was Clarence "Pants" Rowland. The star was a country boy from South Carolina named Joe Jackson, who was known as "Shoeless" because of his poverty-stricken upbringing.

Jackson, who had played previously for the Philadelphia Athletics and the Cleveland Indians, was an outstanding fielder, but he was an even better hitter. No less a superstar than Ty Cobb of the Detroit Tigers called Jackson "the finest natural hitter in the history of the game." A young slugger with the Boston Red Sox named Babe Ruth tried to imitate Jackson's swing. "I copied Jackson's hitting style because I thought he was the greatest hitter I'd ever seen," Ruth explained years later. "I still think the same way." But perhaps the biggest compliment directed toward Jackson may have come from Washington Senators star pitcher Walter Johnson, a man never known to give praise to anyone. "I consider Joe Jackson the greatest natural ballplayer I've ever seen," Johnson claimed.

Led by Jackson, Happy Felsch, and pitchers Eddie Cicotte and Red Faber, the White Sox rolled up one hundred victories in 1917 to win the American League pennant. In the World Series against the powerful New York Giants, the White Sox claimed their second major-league championship by winning the series four games to two. Red Faber started and won two games and also saved a third.

Two years later the mighty Sox were in the World Series again, thanks to pitchers Eddie Cicotte, who won twenty-nine games and lost only seven, and Claude "Lefty" Williams, who won twenty-three games for Chicago. But Cicotte and Williams were ineffective in the World Series, combining to lose five games to the Cincinnati Reds, who won the best-of-nine series five games to three.

A year later Cicotte confessed to accepting a ten-thousand-dollar bribe from gamblers to throw the series. Soon more of the story began to unfold. Supposedly, first baseman Chick Gandil was the White Sox player the gamblers had paid. Gandil then was alleged to have passed the money on to other Chicago players, including Lefty Williams, Happy Felsch, Swede Risberg, Fred McMullin, Buck Weaver, and Joe Jackson.

The eight players, who became known as the "Black Sox," were brought to trial, but were acquitted on all charges of fixing the series. Baseball commissioner Kenesaw Mountain Landis, however, was not convinced the "Black Sox" were innocent. He banned them all from baseball for life. Jackson, who finished his major-league career with a .356 batting average, second only to that of Ty Cobb on the all-time list, never stopped fighting to clear his name.

The star slugger, who could neither read nor write, admitted he took five thousand dollars from Gandil, but then thought about giving the money back. Jackson wanted to turn the money over to Comiskey, but decided against it. If Jackson did try to fix the

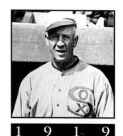

In his first year as manager Kid Gleason led the Sox to a 88–52 record and the AL pennant.

9

Pitcher Eric King.

Fleet-footed Sammy Sosa.   11

series, he went about it in a strange way. He batted .375 during the series, committed no errors, and compiled twelve hits, a World Series record that stood until 1964.

Now, forty years after Jackson's death, some are still trying to clear Shoeless Joe's name and get him inducted into baseball's Hall of Fame. "Joe Jackson has been out of baseball seventy years," wrote Donald Gropman in his biography of Jackson, *Say It Ain't So, Joe!* "Why does he keep popping up? He's a metaphor for something—the Huckleberry Finn of baseball. He had that naïve innocence and was chewed up and spit out. And his ghost has never been quite laid to rest." Jackson, who learned to read and write, and eventually became a successful businessman, went to his grave in 1951 convinced he wasn't guilty. On his deathbed he looked up at his wife and said, "I'm going to meet the greatest umpire of all—and he knows I'm innocent."

After losing such stars as Jackson, Cicotte, Williams, and Weaver, the White Sox fell into a terrible slump, one that would endure through an almost endless succession of losing seasons. There were few highlights during this awful stretch, except for Luke Appling's two batting titles, in 1936 and 1943. The club went through a series of managers: Frank Chance, Ed Collins, Ray Schalk, Owen Bush, Lewis Fonseca, Ted Lyons, and Jack Onslow. Finally, Paul Richards took the helm and began to turn things around. The White Sox led the American League for forty-four days in 1951 before winding up in fourth place. The 1957 team ended the season in third place, the club's highest finish in thirty-seven years.

The Chicago White Sox fans finally had a team with a positive identity—the club was known as the "Go Go White Sox" because of its tremendous speed and base-stealing ability. Shortstop Luis Aparicio, who led the American League in steals in 1956, 1957, 1958, and 1959, and second baseman Nellie Fox, one of the finest natural hitters in the game, formed an awesome double-play combination. Center fielder Jim Landis and first baseman Earl Torgeson hit with power, and pitcher Bill Pierce blazed his fastball past opposing hitters. Knuckleball pitcher Hoyt Wilhelm mystified batters with his fluttering pitch.

The White Sox had become the most entertaining thing to hit the South Side in several years, and new owner Bill Veeck was determined to win the fans over with a show-biz approach. He built a scoreboard in Chicago's Comiskey Park that shot off fireworks, and he

Minnie Minoso made his White Sox debut, thereby becoming the first black player to play for the team.

13

Future Hall-of-Famer Nellie Fox led the "Go Go Sox" with a .306 batting average.

played music when the White Sox made a good play. Veeck amused the fans before games with bareback riders, elephants, sword swallowers, and clowns.

But the White Sox were the most exciting performers on the program in 1959. They were led by manager Al Lopez, pitcher Early Wynn, who won twenty-two games and the American League Cy Young Award, and the league's Most Valuable Player Nellie Fox. The White Sox rolled to a 94–60 record and their first American League pennant in forty years. Chicago then surprised National League champion Los Angeles with an 11–0 victory in the first game of the World Series, but the Dodgers rebounded to take four of the next five to win the series four games to two. Chicago's best season in four decades had ended; unfortunately for South Side fans, it would be twenty-four more years before they would get a chance to cheer another championship team.

Chicago might have been the best team during the 1960s that did not win a pennant. The White Sox finished second in the American League three straight years, from 1963 through 1965. In 1967 Chicago went into the final week of the season with an excellent chance to finish first, but the White Sox faded and lost out to the Boston Red Sox. It was the last time in more than a decade that Chicago would contend for a pennant.

Even though the team faded a bit during the 1970s, several players contributed outstanding individual performances. Third baseman Bill Melton led the American League in home runs in 1971 with thirty-three. The following season Dick Allen, Chicago's star first baseman, topped the league in homers (thirty-seven) and runs batted in (113), and was named the league's Most

Hard throwing Melido Perez.

Bill Melton (with ball), not only led the league in homers (33), but played fine defensively for Chicago.

Valuable Player. Allen also won an American League home-run title in 1974 with thirty-two. Despite the heroics of Allen and Melton, though, the White Sox lagged behind the contenders in the American League's West Division during the 1970s. (In 1969 the American League was split into two divisions, the East and the West.) But the team's fortunes started to change at the end of the 1979 season, when Tony La Russa was named manager.

CARLTON CATCHES ON IN CHICAGO

Led by La Russa and the strong hitting of Chet Lemon and Lamar Johnson, the White Sox raced to the lead in the AL West in the early part of the 1980 season. Chicago, however, faded to fifth place by the end of the season. It was a bitter disappointment to owner Bill

Slugger Dick Allen.

Carlton Fisk

Pitcher LaMarr Hoyt (right), completed his first full season in a White Sox uniform.

Veeck, who then sold the team to real estate baron Jerry Reinsdorf and lawyer Eddie Einhorn. The new owners moved quickly and boldly by signing free-agent catcher Carlton Fisk to a five-year, $2.9-million contract. Fisk, who grew up in the New England area and spent nine years with the Boston Red Sox, was thirty-three years old, almost ancient by catching standards. But Fisk knew how to take care of himself. He maintained a strenuous exercise program that many teammates thought was too taxing. Fisk, however, believed that keeping fit was essential.

"Success has no shortcut, only a high price of pain and humiliation," he explained. "I may seem like some crusty old New Englander, but if you're going to do something, do it right, or don't do it at all." Of his exercise program, Fisk said, "This work has strengthened my legs so that it's actually easier for me to catch today than it was ten years ago. I think this physical commitment has maintained my focus and ability to concentrate. Baseball requires mental strength. The season has a lot of 'give-in' days. The commitment overcomes that."

Despite Fisk's commitment to fitness, he had some difficulty adjusting to being a White Sox player. After all, he had lived most of his life in or near Boston, and most fans still identified Fisk with his heroics as a Red Sox star, which included a dramatic home run in the sixth game of the 1975 World Series. "For the first three years here, every time I'd pass a mirror in my White Sox uniform, I'd think, What's wrong with that picture?" Fisk laughed. "For years being a New Englander and being on the Red Sox were so entwined."

Fisk may not have been totally comfortable in a White Sox uniform, but he was playing as if he had been a Chicagoan all his life. In 1983, his third year as a White Sox player, Fisk slammed twenty-six home runs, drove in eighty-six runs, and batted .330 during the last four months of the season. He also expertly handled a pitching staff that included American League Cy Young Award winner LaMarr Hoyt. The pitchers received offensive help from outfielder Ron Kittle, whose thirty-five homers and one hundred RBI, earned him the American League's Rookie of the Year title. Designated hitter Greg Luzinski chipped in thirty-two homers.

As a result of these performances, the White Sox, who lost twenty-four of their first forty games, rebounded to win the AL West by an astounding twenty games over second-place Kansas City. It was the largest margin of victory in an American League race in nearly fifty years.

1 9 8 0

Brit Burns, the ace of the Chicago staff, led the Sox in wins, ERA and innings pitched.

Ron Kittle.

The architect of the team's success, Tony La Russa, was named the 1983 Manager of the Year.

But La Russa and the White Sox saw their luck run out in the American League Championship Series against Baltimore. The Orioles lost the first game of the best-of-five series, but then rallied for three straight victories to claim the pennant. The White Sox vowed to return to postseason play the following year, but it was not to be. The team went from AL West champs in 1983 to chumps in 1984, posting a 74–88 record, a twenty-five-game slide from the previous season. "I'm just happy the season is over," said a dejected Tony La Russa. Most of the Chicago stars slumped in 1984, but there was one exception—right fielder Harold Baines.

Harold Baines ended the longest game in AL history (25 innings) with a home run.

QUIET BAINES LETS HIS BAT DO THE TALKING

Unlike most stars, Baines wasn't flashy. He didn't talk much, and if it weren't for the fact that he almost always seemed to be playing well, most fans probably wouldn't have noticed him. "He does his job diligently and smoothly, with little fanfare," said White Sox general manager Roland Hemond. "His personality shows up in game-winning situations. People who've been jumping up and down all day have nothing left. Harold's ready." Baines proved his value in clutch situations during the 1983 season, when he set a major-league record with twenty-two game-winning RBI. "In the next ten years," predicted former White Sox owner Bill Veeck, "I think he'll become the premier hitter—and power hitter—in baseball."

24   *Left to right: Dan Pasqua, Harold Baines, Greg Walker, Dave Gallagher.*

Veeck and most baseball experts were impressed with Baines's ability to adjust at the plate. "He has excellent hand-eye coordination," explained Texas Rangers pitcher Frank Tanana. "He'll pick up the pitch right away, tell what kind it is and how fast it's going, and then pop it." Baines believed his batting success was based on studying the opposition. "I'm a guess hitter," he said. "I guess with the catcher because he calls the game. Before I bat I'll watch how the catcher works a hitter they might pitch the same as me, like [Chicago first baseman] Greg Walker. I try not to overswing, and I concentrate harder after the seventh inning."

Unfortunately for Baines and the White Sox, few of his teammates had the ability to concentrate in the late innings during the 1984 season. The team lost thirty-two games by one run in 1984. The White Sox, who led the division at the All-Star break, faded into oblivion after that. Team management was disappointed enough to try to make major changes, one of which was to trade pitching ace LaMarr Hoyt to the San Diego Padres for several young players, including a shortstop named Ozzie Guillen.

1 9 8 5

Tom Seaver won his 300th game in dramatic fashion, before a packed house in Yankee Stadium.

GUILLEN TAKES THE SHORT ROUTE TO STARDOM

Guillen was a natural aquisition for the White Sox, who had a tradition of fine Latin American short-stops. Like Luis Aparicio, the team's great shortstop of the late 1950s and early 1960s, Guillen was born in Venezuela. Although only a rookie, he had the instincts of a veteran in the field. "Ozzie reminds me of Red Schoendienst when he came over to Milwaukee and

Catcher Carlton Fisk ripped his 2000th career hit against New York at Comiskey Park.

solidified the defense in 1957," recalled White Sox general manager Roland Hemond, who played with Schoendienst in Milwaukee. "We'd say, 'What a great fielder, what instinct, what knowledge of the hitters.' But Red was thirty-four; Ozzie's twenty-one."

Opponents also marveled at Guillen's abilities in the field. Kansas City veteran second baseman Frank White claimed Guillen "has all the tools." Guillen worked on his "tools" by practicing his fielding as often as possible, with a mitt that was tiny. "All the great Venezuelan shortstops use the same style as I do in fielding practice," Guillen explained. "They take a small glove and try to catch everything one-handed. That makes your hand strong."

Guillen was also willing to work to strengthen other aspects of his game. In one game in 1985, he drew a walk and then threw his bat in the air, nearly hitting himself on the head. When Guillen reached first base, coach Joe Nossek joked, "We better practice that, Ozzie, so you don't hurt yourself. Be out here early tomorrow." Nossek was making a joke, but Guillen turned to him and said, "What time?"

Guillen's all-around play earned him the American League Rookie of the Year award in 1985. There were no team honors for the White Sox, however, as Chicago could not regain its 1983 form. In fact, the team slumped all the way to last place in 1989, posting the second-worst record in the American League. But out of the ashes of that awful season emerged a new power in 1990. Most experts picked the White Sox to finish last in the seven-team American League West, but Chicago and manager Jeff Torborg had other ideas.

1 9 9 0

Outfielder Sammy Sosa (left) led Chicago to a surprising second place finish in the AL West.

Ozzie Guillen became one of the top hitters in the league. Outfielders Ivan Calderon, Sammy Sosa, and Lance Johnson all hit for power and average. Carlton Fisk had one of the top batting averages on the team, but his most important contribution to the White Sox was handling the club's superb young pitching staff. Starters Eric King, Melido Perez, and Greg Hibbard, all of whom are in their mid-twenties, pitched extremely well in 1990. But their performances were almost second-rate compared with the contributions of Chicago's relief pitchers. Bobby Thigpen, who had one of the top save totals in the American League, made the All-Star team. Barry Jones and Scott Radinsky combined for a 15–1 record during the first half of the 1990 season.

Thanks mostly to a pitching staff that had one of the best earned-run averages in the major leagues, the White

Lance Johnson.

Sox went from losers in 1989 to contenders in 1990. They battled tooth-and-nail with the world-champion Oakland A's for the American League West title. Experts said all year that the team's performance was a fluke, but Chicago stuck with it and made fools out of those experts. The White Sox also made the last year of base-ball in old Comiskey Park a memorable one.

The old ballpark, built in 1910, has been replaced by the "New Comiskey Park." The new stadium is right across the street from old Comiskey, which means the White Sox literally aren't very far from their past. With perhaps one of the most talented young teams in baseball, the White Sox are hoping to rekindle memories of the great Chicago teams of the early years of the American League.